Also by R. Scott Mackey

Ray Courage Mystery Series

Courage Matters

Courage Resurrected

Non-Fiction

Barbary Baseball: The Pacific Coast League of the 1920s

COURAGE BEGINS

A novella by R. Scott Mackey

Big Hound Publishing

Sacramento, CA

For Colby

"It's nice having you on board, Dr. Courage," Alex Melia said, sitting at his office desk. He was the chief investigator for California Farmers Insurance Company. "I have to say you're the oldest intern we've ever had, but your track record at Sac State was impressive."

"Thank you. And, please, call me Ray." After twenty-two years as a professor at Sacramento State University, I retired at age fifty-two. Now, here I was starting a second career as a private investigator with a mandatory internship. "I appreciate your company accepting an old fart like me into your internship program."

Melia was a small man, with fine features and dark, lank hair he occasionally swept away from his eyes. I put him at forty, give or take. He said he'd been at California Farmers ever since he graduated from Sac State seventeen years before, and had risen through the ranks to his current position.

"Normally, our interns shadow our more seasoned investigators for the first few weeks," he said. "But with your, well, life experience, we thought it might be best to give you an actual assignment to work on your own."

"That sounds good to me." The path to becoming a private investigator required a minimum of four thousand hours of paid investigative work. I wanted to get that as soon as possible so I could start my own investigation agency. Getting my own case at Cal Farm might enable me to work long days to build up my hourly count.

"We have several non-active case files that our fulltime investigators just don't have time to revisit. They're cases that have cost the firm a lot of money in insurance payouts, but which we think might be fraudulent."

He picked up a manila folder from a stack on his desk, flipped it open, and leafed through it. He nodded as he read, then shut the file and slid it across the desk to me.

"This policy cost us one and a half million dollars. We think it's bunk, but none of our investigators could prove it. The police couldn't prove it either."

"The police? What kind of a case is it?"

"It was ruled an accidental death. But the circumstances suggest it might be homicide. A murder."

I picked up the file. A murder investigation was much different than my previous life evaluating freshman speeches, grading midterms, and listening to blowhard professors boast about their brilliance during staff meetings.

"Tiffanie Bate," I said. "I remember this one from the news. She died about two years ago. Carbon monoxide poisoning."

2

"Yeah. Twenty-six years old. Married four years to Garrett Bate. One month before her death, he opened up a one point five million dollar life insurance policy on her. Days after he buries poor old Tiffanie he's seen all over town dating a stripper named Candy Cane from Showtime Starlets."

"Wasn't the wife found dead with her lover? She was cheating on him."

"Yeah, but she didn't deserve what she got. And it does suggest motive for a jealous husband."

When I peeked into the file for the first time, my heart started to pound. This was real. Going into the private investigation field hadn't been a lark, but it had been almost theoretical on my part, a decision made clinically when I did a self-evaluation of my skills and the professions where they might prove useful.

Holding that file, I felt its weight—literally and figuratively. The file detailed the death of a woman killed before she'd had a chance to truly live. The responsibility to do right by her slapped me across the face. I owed Tiffanie Bate my best effort. To determine if somebody had deliberately killed her or if she had indeed died accidentally. I took two deep breaths to calm myself. My heart continued to thump hard against my chest.

"Is there any proof that he killed her?" The file was almost two inches thick. It would take me a while to get through it.

"No, none. And he has a perfect alibi. I'd just like to nail the smug SOB."

2

I was sitting at Say Hey's bar, nursing a glass of Rubicon IPA and reading through the file on Tiffanie Bate, when Rubia approached me from the other side of the counter.

"You going to drink that beer or wait until it evaporates?"

"I'm working," I said.

"Last I heard, you quit working when you walked out the door at Sac State."

"Very funny."

Rubia. The woman with a longshoreman's mouth, a nun's heart, and a preference for action over analysis. She'd been a student of mine at Sacramento State University. An ex-gangbanger, she was a petite Latina, festooned with tattoos up and down both arms. She had a feistiness two years of prison couldn't break. She decided to go straight after seeing the perilous path gang life promised, earning her bachelor's degree in communication studies in just three years. I considered her not only one of my top former students, but also one of my best friends. Two years after graduating from college, she inherited the Say Hey, a small bar in Sacramento's Land Park neighborhood, from her uncle.

"You really going to do this private investigator shit?"

I looked at her reproachfully over the top of my reading glasses.

"Okay, you really going to do this private investigator *stuff*?"

"That's better." I'd been trying to clean up her language ever since she set foot in my class years before.

"Hey, you want your key back?" she asked.

"Nah. Go ahead and keep it." I'd given her a key a few weeks before so she could check on my house when I was down in LA visiting my daughter.

"I might have a wild-assed party at your place next time you leave town."

"Knock yourself out." I turned my attention back to the folder.

"What's that you're working on?"

"A suspicious death. Or at least the insurance company thinks it's suspicious."

"Isn't this bullshit, er, subject matter, a little out of your league?"

"You underestimate me. This isn't much harder than dealing with twenty year olds who claim they left their assignment at home after putting out a house fire, burying their grandmother, and performing CPR on their dog."

"I used that one once."

"Why do you think I used it as an example?"

"So what's the case?" Rubia picked up my half-full glass, set it under a beer tap, topped it off, and returned it to me.

"A woman named Tiffanie Bate died in her Tahoe vacation home from carbon monoxide poisoning. The husband received a million and a half on a policy he'd just opened on her. He got what she had in the bank, and their homes in Tahoe and Sacramento reverted to his sole ownership. In all, he cleared more than three million dollars."

"I remember that. It was in the news. She was banging somebody in the house. They both died, right?"

I nodded. "Guy's name was Harley Cowan. He was a building contractor up in Tahoe. Apparently, Ms. Bate and he were a regular thing. She'd go up to Tahoe to go 'skiing' or 'hiking' and spend her days and nights in intimate relations with Mr. Cowan."

"So that's why hubby wanted to kill the bitch, I mean his wife."

"That's the theory. The problem is that Garrett Bate was giving a speech in Sacramento at the time they were killed. He said he hadn't been up to Tahoe in months, and nobody can prove him wrong."

The Kings and Bulls were playing a preseason game on the television at the end of the bar. A spectacular dunk by the Kings's center caught my attention, and I wanted to watch the replay before continuing the conversation. I watched the dunk three times in slow motion and sipped my beer.

Rubia went to the end of the bar to serve two new customers. I reflected on how much my life had changed in the past couple of months, and especially in the few hours since getting this case. The last six or seven years of my teaching career I felt I was living on autopilot. I didn't love teaching anymore. My days at work became a sleepwalk. I'd entered academia to teach and discover. At the end I was doing very little of either. The world was passing me by. Becoming an investigator seemed like a way to jumpstart my sensibilities and connect with life again, in a world altogether different from the one I just left.

"What's this Garrett do?" Rubia asked, returning after serving the customers, snapping me back to the moment.

"He's a senior manager at his family's real estate company. The night of the accident, or whatever you want to call it, he was giving a speech at the Sacramento Realtors Awards Night. We have employees, clients, and even competitive real estate agents who swear they were in face-to-face contact with him all day. Not only that, the police have signed affidavits from numerous witnesses that he was in Sacramento every day for at least two weeks before the day of the killing."

"Maybe it was an accident after all."

"That's what I was thinking, too," I said. "It's just that it looked like someone had punched a hole in the heater's flue

7

exhaust stack and put some residue just above it to partially block it. That would have released the CO into the house to kill them. A few months before, Garrett had some work done on the house to make it more energy efficient. He installed more insulation, triple-paned windows, caulked all the outlets, and so on. Basically, he made the house more airtight, so that outside air was tougher to get in. And inside air couldn't get out."

"Good way to keep the carbon monoxide inside."

"Yep."

"So the dude might have done it."

"Maybe. But his alibi is bulletproof."

3

Garrett Bate greeted me with a fake smile, revealing perfectly straight teeth as white as a puppy's. He looked dashing in cream cotton pants; a blue Ralph Lauren button-down, sleeves rolled up to mid-forearm; and a light sweater draped over his shoulders and tied loosely at the neck. He was tall; at six foot four, he stood two inches taller than me, with a trim, athletic build, gray eyes, and thick brown hair. He'd just stepped out of a dark green Jaguar XF in front of the Bate Real Estate office on Fair Oaks Boulevard, the stretch of road known as "Sacramento's Rodeo Drive."

"Looking for a new house?" he asked as I approached, mistaking me for a potential client. He shut the driver's door and opened the rear passenger's door, retrieving an alligator briefcase no bigger than a pad of paper. "You've come to the right place. We're the best in town."

I offered my hand, which he shook with a bit too much familiarity, holding the grip a tad too long. His eyes locked on mine until I had to look away. In those few seconds, I could tell he was secure in his good looks and imbued with a sense of superiority. But despite the Hollywood exterior, he exuded a reptilian core that leaked through those cold gray eyes. It made me want to shudder.

"My name's Ray Courage. I'm an investigator with Cal Farm Insurance."

That wiped the fake smile off his face. He rolled his shoulders once before using his key fob to lock the car. "What can I do for you?" He tried to sound helpful, but his voice couldn't hide his irritation.

"I just had a few questions about the Tahoe accident. My belated condolences, by the way." I'd suffered the loss of my wife more than ten years before and still missed her.

He gave a slight nod and then looked in the direction of his office. It was early March, and the valley fog painted a bleak landscape, a gray world of blurred shapes and muted reality. "I have a client waiting inside, so this really isn't the best time. Besides, I already answered your company's questions. The settlement's been paid. Case closed. End of story."

"Probably so. We're just trying to clear up some loose ends to make everything as neat as you describe it." I pulled out a memo pad and a pen. "Where did you say you were the night of the accident?"

He rolled his eyes and shook his head, a petulant six-year-old. "Really? We have to do this all over again? Is your company reopening its investigation? Because if you are, then I think I'll contact my lawyer."

"Just need to confirm a couple of things. For the record."

"You already have the record. Oh, for God's sake, to get you out of my hair, I'll repeat what I told you guys two years ago. I was giving a speech to four hundred real estate agents at the Crocker Art Museum. Before and after the speech, I was seated at one of the front tables. The event ended just before eleven o'clock. Afterwards, we went to Ella Restaurant for some cocktails. I had a bit too much to drink, so I rented a room at the Hyatt on L Street. Security cameras show me checking in about one in the morning, and checking out at about eight the following morning, after having a room service breakfast at seven. I did not leave my room between those hours, as security cameras have confirmed. Now are you happy?"

His account was identical to the testimony he'd given two years before. "I know you have to meet someone in your office. How about I walk with you to save you some time?"

"I'd rather you not." He started towards the office a hundred feet across the parking lot. I followed.

We passed a red Mercedes E350, out of which emerged an attractive older woman. "Good morning, Garrett," she said.

"Mom."

"We need to talk when you get a chance, about the Thompson listing." She looked at me. She was medium height, slender, her stylish dark hair accented with streaks of gray. She wore a long black skirt and a mottled gray and white collared sweater.

When her son didn't immediately introduce us, I did so myself.

"Amanda Bate," she said, shaking my hand. Her eyes worked me up and down in a way that almost made me blush.

"Is Mr. Courage one of your clients, Garrett?"

"No, we're just having a friendly chat." He gave me an exaggerated smile.

"Nice to meet you, Mr. Courage." She smiled at me before excusing herself and heading towards the office.

"You could have introduced us," I said. "Making me do it myself. Makes me feel cheap and easy."

He glared at me. So much for lightening the mood.

"Does your dad work in the office as well?" I gestured with my chin towards the office.

"No. My mom and dad have been divorced since I was twelve. He has nothing to do with our company."

"Oh, sorry. Anyway, where were we? Oh, yeah, you couldn't have been in Tahoe at the time of your wife's death because you were in Sacramento."

"Yes. So that completes this conversation." He started to walk off.

"Were you and your wife having marital difficulties?" It was a pointed, if not downright rude, question, but a shot I needed to take. I'd already decided I didn't like the man. And the odds of us becoming steady lunch pals seemed remote, so I didn't see the downside to being a bit of a jerk if it might get him to say something incriminating.

"No."

"No? She was killed while having a tryst with another man. And you were seeing other women. Or so I'm told."

He didn't bother to look at me as we strode through the fog. "We were not having difficulties."

"The report indicates that you were."

"The report is wrong. My wife and I loved each other. And I'm getting sick and tired of you—and your company—implying that I had anything to do with the unfortunate accident that killed her."

"You can see from our point of view that—"

"I don't see shit from your point of view! What I see is a multibillion-dollar company that makes more money each year than the GNP of most counties, trying to harass one of its customers. I paid my premiums, and it was your obligation to pay me what I was due."

I didn't know what to say to that. If he hadn't been such an arrogant prick, I might have agreed with him. Maybe what I was doing was harassment, especially if he was telling the truth. We walked in silence for a few seconds.

"What did you talk about?" I asked.

"What?"

"Your speech. What was it about?"

He stopped to look at me. A haughty smile crossed his face. "You should watch it for yourself. It's on YouTube. It was a humorous speech. I got a standing ovation for it."

With that, he pulled open the glass front door and entered the office, leaving me standing outside in the fog.

4

The drive up from the valley floor, through the rolling foothills and up into the Sierra Nevada Mountain Range, took a little over two hours. The mid-week traffic, light on Interstate 80, enabled me to cruise at a comfortable seventy miles an hour almost the entire trip. The depressing fog of the valley gave way to bright blue skies at Lake Tahoe. It was a spectacular day, the temperature in the low thirties on a windless, early afternoon.

Times must have been good at the lake. Dozens of construction crews worked on houses, either building new ones or remolding old ones, as people invested in upgrades to their homes. Quite a contrast to the recent recession in which owners dumped vacation homes at fire-sale prices. What a boon to the local construction trades.

I'd phoned the offices of Crane and Crane and got an address from the woman who answered. Pulling on a jacket, after emerging from my car, I found a crew working on the house I'd been looking for.

Two men stood in front of a partially-framed new home, looking over blueprints spread on the hood of a pickup truck. Three more men worked inside the house, their efforts filling the mountain air with the harsh whine of a buzz saw and the rat-tat-tat of dueling hammers.

"Is one of you Billy Crane?" I asked, raising my voice above the din.

They looked at me warily, decked out in white hard hats, sweatshirts, and blue jeans. "Who wants to know?" the short man asked.

I introduced myself, explaining that I worked for Cal Farm Insurance.

"I'm Billy," the same man said. "What can I do for you?"

Billy shook my hand; thick calluses lined his palm and fingers. It was like grasping a catcher's mitt. He reeked of tobacco and sweat, the odors mixing with those of the fresh cut wood and pine trees. If testosterone had a smell, it would be this.

"What brings you all this way from Sacramento?" Though Billy was short, he outweighed me by a good thirty pounds. He sported a three-day growth of stubble and had a pinch of tobacco in his lower lip.

"We're still looking into the Bate accident from a couple of years ago. You know, the carbon monoxide poisoning."

"Yeah, you don't have to remind me. I know that one all too well. Lost one of my best men in that deal."

"Harley Cowan was one of your employees?" That hadn't been in the case file.

"Yes, sir. Damn good finish carpenter. Those are hard to find. Just couldn't keep his pecker in his pants, and it cost him."

"How long had he been seeing Mrs. Bate?"

"Hell if I know. "

"Did it start when you began doing the improvements on the Bate home?"

"Like I said, I don't have a clue. He could've met her years before for all I know. Bate and his wife had been coming up here for a while."

I considered pursuing Cowan's connection to Tiffanie Bate, but didn't see where that could take me. "Do you mind if I ask you a few questions about the work you did on the Bate home?"

"Sure, go ahead. I got nothing to hide." He spit some tobacco juice on the dirt next to the truck's tire.

"When did Garrett Bate call you, and what did he ask you to do at the house?"

"Hell, I don't remember exactly when he called me. It was, maybe, a month before we started doing work on his house, sometime in late summer. I remember because he was in a hurry. He got a little ticked when I told him we couldn't start on his house until the next spring."

"Why the delay?"

"Because we was crazy busy."

"But you said he contacted you about a month before you started."

"Yeah," he said, laughing at some recollection. "He said he'd pay twice our going rate if we could get his work done by Thanksgiving. Said he wanted to enjoy the winter season comfortably. Offer like that makes you put other jobs on the back burner."

"What exactly did he want you to do at the house?"

"He wanted to make it energy efficient. It's pretty mild today, but the winters can get brutal up here. He was tired of

16

freezing his ass off and said to spare no expense. We sealed up that sumbitch like nobody's business."

"Did you think his request was unusual?"

"No, not really. It costs a lot of money to keep your home warm up here in the winter. The kind of stuff we did to his house was expensive, but in the long run, he'd make most of the money back in energy savings. Plus, he'd have a more comfortable place to live."

"You put in more insulation and that kind of stuff, right?"

"You name it, we did it. Triple-pane storm windows throughout—that was the big expense. Thicker insulation in the walls and attic, eliminated the gaps under the outside doors, caulking, weather stripping, and a few other things."

"What about the furnace? Did you install a new furnace for him?"

Billy spit again. "No, that's the crazy thing. I told him it would be smarter, and cost less, to heat the place with a pellet-stove system. He said he preferred the furnace. So I told him the one he had was over twenty years old, and that the newer models were ten times more efficient. And his was loud, too, sitting there in the hallway across from his bedroom. Hell, that change alone might have saved him more than everything else we did. He didn't care. He said he wanted to keep the old furnace."

"The furnace that leaked and ended up killing his wife."

"Yep. Sure was. Damn shame."

5

Detective Harrison Royle of the Tahoe Police Department met me at the Jack in the Box in South Lake Tahoe. I arrived first and ordered some chicken nuggets and a cup of coffee. At mid-afternoon, I was the only customer sitting in the restaurant. Harrison spotted me and sat at the table, declining my offer to buy him something to eat or drink.

"I'm not going to have much to tell you," he said, soon after we'd introduced ourselves.

I was starving, not having time to stop after talking with Garrett Bate and leaving for Lake Tahoe to meet Billy Crane. I dipped one of the chicken nuggets into a plastic tub of spicy ranch dressing and devoured the morsel in two bites. I followed that with a sip of black coffee. Royle watched me with surprising interest. He was young, late twenties or early thirties, with a shaved head a lot of young men sported to conceal premature baldness. I didn't quite get the logic in that, but had seen it many times in my teaching days.

"Sorry, I missed lunch," I said.

"Is Cal Farm really reopening its investigation of the Tiffanie Bate and Harley Cowan deaths?"

I nodded, starting in on a second chicken nugget.

"Seems like a stretch to me," he said. "No offense, but you guys looked into it as thoroughly as we did back when it happened. I'd think your resources would be better spent elsewhere." Royle had a weariness in his eyes, suggesting he'd seen more in his thirty years than others had seen in sixty.

I swallowed the nugget. "I'm an intern making twenty bucks an hour, so it's not like we're exactly throwing money away."

"An intern? Aren't you a little old to be an intern?"

"Thank you. It's a long story. A career change thing."

"What were you before you were an intern?"

"College professor."

He blinked and scrunched his face. "Isn't interning as an investigator a step down from college professor? No offense meant."

"None taken. Like I said, it's a long story."

He reached down and pulled out a folder from a nylon briefcase. "I brought the case file." He handed it to me.

I wiped my hands on a napkin before taking the packet from him. It was a couple of inches thick. "Anything particularly noteworthy in here?"

"Not really. Probably contains pretty much everything you have in your file."

The papers had two holes punched in the top and connected to the folder with metal prongs. I scanned through the pages, flipping them up as I went. I stopped to read more closely when I came to the South Lake Tahoe Arson Unit's report. I'd skimmed the same report in our files before, but wanted to see if something jumped out this time around. Nothing did. The report concluded the blockage in the furnace's flue exhaust stack, coupled with a puncture hole in the stack beneath the obstruction, caused carbon monoxide to escape and eventually fill the home with enough of the gas to kill the occupants. The investigator called the location and size of the blockage and hole suspicious, but offered no evidence that the stack had been tampered with. An autopsy report confirmed both victims died from carbon monoxide poisoning.

"What did you think about the blockage and hole they found?" I asked.

Royle shrugged. "It was an old furnace. Residue builds up. As far as the hole, someone could have accidentally punctured it doing routine repairs. Then, over time, pressure from the exhaust expanded the hole."

"Do you believe that?"

"No, I think somebody stuffed a bunch of soot in there. Then they punctured it with a screwdriver and widened the size of the hole with a pair of pliers."

I raised my eyebrows at the specificity of his theory.

He turned both palms up and shrugged again. "Hey, that's how I would've done it. That's all."

"Was there any physical evidence putting Garrett at the scene?"

"Yeah, his fingerprints were all over the place. Same with hair and skin. But it was his house, and he'd been inside a few months before. There were no prints or anything suggesting he'd been inside the utility closet where the furnace was."

I leafed through a couple more pages, and then came upon color photos inserted into a plastic sleeve. "Okay if I look at the pics?"

"Suit yourself."

I took out an eight-by-ten print of the bedroom. A blonde woman lay face down in a bed, the green comforter drawn partly back to expose a bare shoulder and arm. Next to her lay a man face up, his eyes closed. They could've been sleeping. I showed the photo to Royle.

He nodded. "Dead. That's how we found them. We got a call at nine thirty that morning from Harley Cowan's dad. The kid hadn't shown up for work, so Billy Crane calls the dad—Cowan lived at home. Dad said he hasn't seen the kid, so he starts looking for him by driving around and sees Harley's pickup at the Bate house. He's pissed when no one answers, figures his son is having sex with the woman instead of going to work, so he finds an open side door and enters. Five minutes later he calls us."

I no longer had any interest in my chicken nuggets. Even looking at them, and the tub of ranch, made me feel queasy, so I closed the box and slid it to the edge of the table. I put the photo back in the sleeve and pulled out a couple more. They didn't reveal anything new, just the same scene from different angles. The last photograph showed a close-up of the hole in the flue stack. I had to admit, Royle's description of how the hole could've been created seemed spot on.

"Do you have the surveillance video from the Hyatt in Sacramento?" I asked. Cal Farm's file lacked the actual video footage. Our report relied on the written description of the video provided by the Tahoe Police, stating Garrett Bate was the subject captured on camera the night of his wife's death.

"Yeah, Sac PD helped us a lot with this one. They went through all the videos from the Hyatt and sent us digital files. It took a few weeks with all the footage and red tape with the hotel. I personally reviewed everything and wrote the report. I can forward you a link to the video if you want."

I told him I'd like to see what they had and gave him my e-mail address. "Our file says the coroner put the time of death at midnight."

"Plus or minus an hour, but certainly within that window."

The timeframe bothered me as much as anything. Even if Bate had been able to leave immediately after the real estate awards at the Crocker, there was no way he could get to Tahoe in time to tamper with the furnace's gas line. Hell, they might have been dead about the time the event ended.

"Could Bate have tampered with the furnace earlier, like a day or two, or even a week before?" Bate supposedly had an alibi for a couple of weeks leading up to the deaths, but he could've sneaked out at night and returned the next morning.

"No. All our experts agree that the hole would have leaked enough carbon monoxide to kill anyone in that house running the furnace for more than a couple of hours. Tiffanie had been staying there for almost a full week. If the tampering had been done earlier, she would've suffered from the CO poisoning before she did."

"Maybe she didn't turn on the heater."

Royle shook his head. "It was cold as hell that week. She probably ran the heater non-stop while she was there. The PG&E meter records confirmed that."

I thought I'd been coming up with new possibilities, but the police and the Cal Farm investigators had already explored every angle I'd imagined. So much for my cleverness.

"What about a hired gun, so to speak? He could've paid someone to go inside the house, when Mrs. Bate was out during the day, and tamper with the furnace."

"We looked at that hard. Went through all of his bank records and assets. He hadn't taken more than forty dollars at a time out of an ATM in over a year. No major transactions in any of his accounts. Other than his two houses and the cars, he didn't own anything major. We confirmed, with their homeowner's

23

insurance company, they didn't own any expensive jewelry, except for Mrs. Bate's wedding and engagement rings. We're still monitoring his finances in case he, you know, deferred payments, but so far nada. We even put our best snitches here at the lake to work on it, but they said there was nothing on the street about someone doing a number on that furnace."

"Could've been an outside guy."

Royle reached over and grabbed one of my nuggets. "Do you mind?" He held it up, and I shrugged. "There's a slim chance that happened. But again, no indication that anyone, from anywhere, has been paid. I just don't see it."

"Were there any other suspects besides Bate?"

"We talked to everyone they knew up here, and nobody had a motive to kill either one of them—Tiffanie or Harley. We talked to several people at Bate Real Estate, but that was a dead end. In Sacramento, Tiffanie Bate didn't have any enemies we could find, or anyone who'd benefit from her death."

I turned to the last page of the file, a sheet of lined notebook paper on which someone had written "Miscellaneous." "Is this your handwriting?"

Royle craned his neck to look across the table. "Yeah, those are my notes. I always jot down any random things that come up during an investigation. There's nothing that's worth a damn."

I skimmed the sheet anyway, stopping about halfway down the page at a one-sentence notation. *"Tom Oberto says he spotted*

the suspect on the eight hundred block of Seventh Avenue in the
Tahoma neighborhood at seven o'clock the night of the murder."
I turned the file around so Royle could see it. "What's this?"

"Nothing," he said with a snort after reading it. "Tom is a
local drunk, who also happens to believe in every conspiracy
theory on the market. We get a call from him two, three times a
month, claiming he knows for certain this neighbor or that is
making crystal meth. He heard about the deaths, came to the
conclusion the husband did it, and in a drunken stupor, called us.
Even if he had spotted Bate, Tom isn't credible. Lacking a
corroborating witness, his testimony is crap."

6

I spent the night in Tahoe, looking for Tom Oberto in every
drinking establishment in the west and south sides at the lake. I
started at Sunnyside, where the bartender had never heard of
Oberto. I had no guarantees he'd be out drinking; he could've
been a stay-at-home drinker. Yet Royle made it sound like
Oberto was a local crackpot, known to the community at large.
People like that tended to do their drinking where they had an
audience. Nothing popped when I did a web search for him on
my cell phone. No phone number, no address, no digital or social
media footprint at all. If he was the conspiracy theorist Royle
described, then it made sense Oberto had disconnected from the
digital world.

When I walked into the Fat Cat Bar and Grill, I'd pretty much exhausted all the local watering holes. I'd not had a drop to drink at any of the other bars, but decided I'd order a beer and think about whether to give the east and north shores a shot as well. It would make for a long night, but it was better than staying through the next night, or giving up on Tom Oberto altogether.

I settled on a stool at the end of the bar, where about ten of us sat, all men, all middle aged or younger. The bar curved at both ends, with eight seats in the middle and two seats on the curved ends facing one another. Directly opposite me, on the far end of the bar, a man wearing a green baseball cap and red flannel shirt spoke in a loud voice.

"I'm telling you those Arab motherfuckers are out to take over our way of life," baseball cap guy said, loud enough that his words were clear even across the bar. "I saw one of them ragheads the other day at the store buying a *Penthouse* and a bottle of Jack Daniels. What the fuck? They say they're all about religious purity—jihad and all that shit—and he's out getting lit up and jacking off to an American chick. What's up with that?"

The bartender came over, and I ordered an Eel River IPA on draft. He set the beer glass in front of me. "Who's that guy over there in the A's hat?"

"Tommy O." He didn't turn to look at whom I was referring. "Sorry if he's bugging you. He gets a couple of drinks in him, and there's no switching him off."

"No problem. Just curious."

Oberto continued to spout off about various topics ranging from the Internal Revenue Service, the NFL, anti-gun crusaders, and the Animal Liberation Front. He was a man with a remarkable ability to insult everybody, no matter their politics, race, or religion. His rants effectively cleared the barstools next to him, leaving him to share his opinions solely with himself. I picked up my beer and sauntered over to a barstool two seats away, nodding a hello at him as I sat down.

"What do you think about that?" he asked.

"Sorry?" I'd missed his latest topic during my journey across the bar.

"Global warming. Crock of shit, right?"

Despite my desire to argue the science with him, I demurred. "Right." I held up my beer to him, prompting Oberto to do the same.

"Name's Tom Oberto. But you can call me Tommy, or Tommy O. That's what everyone calls me." Oberto was overweight with a big, red, drinker's nose and a puffy face decorated with a scraggly gray beard.

"Nice to meet you. My name's Ray."

"You're not from around here are you?"

"No, just up for the day."

"Business?"

"Yeah. In fact, you can probably help me out in that regard."

"Me? How?"

I got up and moved to the barstool next to his, leaning in to him conspiratorially. "Do you know a guy named Garrett Bate?"

"Yeah, I know the fucker. Stiffed me a couple of years ago on a job. I cleared nearly half an acre of underbrush and hauled it away. We agreed on four hundred for the job and he gave me two. Said the job took me half the time I said it would. Son of a bitch. He screws me for doing a kick-ass job."

I shook my head in sympathy. "I'm actually here looking into the accident at his house that killed his wife and Harley Cowan two years ago."

"You a cop?"

"Investigator for an insurance company."

He looked at me, nodded, and picked up his shot glass, knocking back the remaining amber liquid. He chased that with several long pulls from a bottle of Bud Light.

"You know, I told the cops back then it wasn't no accident. That son of a bitch Garrett did it sure as day. I saw him that night, not fifty feet from the house. Dressed all in black. He tried to turn his face when I walked by, but I knew it as him. Even in the dark, there was enough moonlight for me to be sure it was him."

"But the cops didn't believe you, did they?"

"They don't believe nothing I say. If they did, the drug problem up here would be fixed overnight. I could tell you each and every meth dealer who lives here. But the cops don't listen to me."

"But you were sure it was Garrett Bate you saw that night?"

"Absolutely. I'd swear to it."

"I mean no offense when I ask you this, but had you been drinking that night when you saw him?"

"Yeah, so what? I drink every night. Doesn't do squat to my eyesight or my memory. That's why I was walking home, because I didn't want to drive after having a few."

7

After leaving the Fat Cat, I drove to my hotel, a Howard Johnson's in South Shore, where I planned to spend the night and then return early the next day to Sacramento.

Detective Royle had been right. Tommy Oberto was a drunk and a crackpot. He seemed the kind of guy who wanted to be the center of attention, someone who'd appear at every crime scene, or car accident, claiming to have witnessed it or having intimate knowledge of what had transpired. I could see a defense lawyer completely discrediting him if he ever found his way to a witness stand. Yet, something made me believe him about seeing Garrett Bate. That by itself counted for nothing.

Oberto's claim did inject me with an ounce of promise. I'd been growing disillusioned over my assignment, believing it might be little more than busy work, to keep me from getting underfoot with the real investigators in the office.

I flipped open my laptop and opened my e-mail. As promised, Royle sent me a link to a Tahoe Police video site along with a guest password for logging in. I clicked on the link, logged in, and watched a two-year-old video of Garrett Bate entering the Hyatt Regency lobby from the second floor of the covered parking deck. The date and time were stamped in the lower left corner of the frame and showed him entering the Hyatt at one thirteen in the morning. That shot cut away, and another camera picked him up as he walked through an upper lobby to a descending escalator. A third shot showed him registering at the front desk and proceeding to an elevator. The next shot in the sequence captured him getting out of the elevator, walking down a hallway, entering his room, and closing the door behind him at one twenty-one.

Time-lapsed images of the hallway showed quick clips of other hotel guests and employees coming and going during the night and early the next morning. The time-lapse sequence turned to regular speed just after seven in the morning, when a room service attendant entered Bate's room with a cart of food. The video fast-forwarded to eight eleven as Bate was leaving his room and entering the elevator.

I watched it all again, and then a third time, looking for something incongruous with what Garrett Bate had told me that morning. Nothing seemed out of the ordinary, except Bate said he'd been too drunk to drive. He didn't appear to be noticeably drunk in the video. Then again, maybe he held his liquor well and was smart enough not to risk driving with even a modest amount of alcohol in his system. I wondered why he didn't call a cab, or Uber, for a ride home rather than fork over two hundred dollars for a night alone in a hotel.

Bate said his speech at the awards ceremony had been recorded and posted on YouTube. I went to the website and found the link. The video was probably from a cell phone camera, the image shaky and dark. Though I'd taken a quick dislike to Garrett Bate, I found his speech engaging. He delivered a hilarious fifteen-minute monologue about the perils of different types of real estate clients, ranging from bimbo trophy wife number two, to gay couples, to the demanding matrons who think every decorating touch is too tacky, and every listing too expensive. He skillfully covered the topic in a way that was edgy yet tasteful, a perfect balance for a professional audience lubricated with copious amounts of wine.

As I watched the video a second time, I compared Bate's YouTube appearance with that on the security feed. As far as I could tell, his hair, mustache, chin beard, and suit matched. When the YouTube video faded to black, a sidebar on the page showed a link to another video from that night entitled "Gracie Nixon Wins Top Agent Award." I launched it.

The camera pointed at a large round table, where Bate and nine others sat. Crystal goblets of wine, and plates of partially eaten dessert, sat atop a white linen tablecloth. White and purple tulips in a cut crystal vase comprised the simple, tasteful centerpiece.

The men dressed in tuxedos or suits, while most of the women wore elegant evening dresses accented with ornate dangling earrings and sparkling necklaces. Bate sat next to a lady in a red dress who was in deep conversation with the man seated on her other side. I couldn't take my eyes off the woman. Her form-fitting dress and blonde hair, pulled into an up-do, accentuated her cheekbones and slender neck, a look at once beautiful and classy. She was whispering into her companion's ear as an unseen emcee made his announcement.

"And the winner is…" The emcee paused for dramatic effect. "From Bate Real Estate, Gracie Nixon!"

Bate looked over his left shoulder as if searching for Gracie. To his right, the woman in the red dress looked stunned for a couple of seconds, both hands covering her mouth. Then came tears and a warm embrace from her male companion. By now, Bate had turned his attention to them. His face didn't display elation, jealousy, or any other emotion. He did shake Gracie's hand when she stood to receive her award. The clip ended just after she pumped her fist once and strode towards the dais wearing a smile of pure joy.

8

Gracie Nixon, Amanda Bate, and Garrett Bate all worked for Bate Real Estate. How did Garrett not know Gracie Nixon sat next to him? They did work in different offices, he in Fair Oaks, and she, several miles away in Curtis Park. Could that explain Garrett's glancing around after her name was called?

I phoned Gracie upon returning to Sacramento after my night in Tahoe, telling her I was interested in one of her real estate listings. If I mentioned the real reason I wanted to talk with her, I feared she'd decline. Speaking to an investigator trying to pin a murder rap on the boss might not, in her mind, be the smartest career move.

I stood on the sidewalk in front of a house facing the leafy and tranquil Curtis Park. The park was much smaller than Land Park, with its soccer, rugby, and baseball fields, golf course, zoo, two small theme parks, picnic areas, and multiple ponds and fountains. Curtis Park had none of that. Its smaller size, and less foot-and-vehicle traffic, made it something of an urban sanctuary, a place for runners, walkers, sleepers, and sunbathers.

The house had a Bate Real Estate sign in the front yard, with Gracie Nixon's name and phone number printed on it. Like many of the homes in the neighborhood, this one was made of old

English brick with a steep roofline of Spanish tiles. From the web page, I knew it was a three bedroom, two bath, with just over eighteen hundred feet of space.

Gracie pulled up in an ice-white Acura Legend. What was it with these real estate agents and their fancy cars?

"Mr. Courage?"

"Please, call me Ray."

"Gracie." We shook hands, and she immediately started searching inside her purse for something, pulling out a key with a satisfied "Aha!"

The YouTube video hadn't done her justice. Though she looked beautiful in the red cocktail dress that night, she was even more gorgeous in person, with long blonde hair, blue eyes, and an engaging smile. She looked in shape, a figure sculpted at the intersection of Pilates and Crossfit.

She led me to the front door, where she used the key to open a lockbox on the door handle. A few moments later, we were inside.

"As you can see, hardwood floors throughout. A recently updated kitchen, which we'll see in a second."

The house was completely empty of furnishings or floor coverings; the only remaining touch from the previous owner appeared to be the drapes hanging in the picture window facing the park.

"You said on the phone you were looking to downsize? Where do you live now?"

"I'm over in Land Park in a four bedroom with three baths. It's more house than I need, now that it's just me." It wasn't an outright lie. I had been thinking about moving into something smaller ever since my daughter Sara had gone off to college four years ago. Now she was admitted into UCLA's law school for the fall, making it doubtful she'd come home to roost anytime soon. I had no prospects for expanding my household other than my occasional urge to get a dog.

We walked through the kitchen with its Wolf range, Sub-Zero refrigerator-freezer, and other appliances that were well beyond my minimal prep, storage and cooking requirements. She showed me the master bedroom and its remodeled bath, the other two bedrooms, dining room, living room, and the second bath— also remodeled.

"What do you think?" she asked as we arrived back at the foyer.

"It's all very nice." I made a show of sweeping my eyes from living room to dining room, rubbing my chin with one hand as I did so. Then I looked at her with mock surprise. "I've seen you before. Two years ago. I was at a real estate awards event at the Crocker. You were Realtor of the Year!"

She blushed, smiling. "Actually, Agent of the Year. Realtor is a whole different category. What were you doing there that night?"

I hadn't thought that far ahead. "Well, my, um, girlfriend at the time was a real estate agent, and I was there with her."

"Oh. Well, thank you for remembering that. It was a big night for me."

"I noticed you were sitting with Garrett Bate. Must have been nice, winning the award with one of the bosses sitting at the table."

She paused a moment, as if trying to bring up the memory. "Oh, yeah, I was. I'd almost forgotten."

"Do you work closely with him?"

"Garrett?"

"Yes."

"No, not at all. At least not now. Back then, more, because I worked out of the Fair Oaks office. That's the main office."

Our conversation shifted to the house again. The price. The neighborhood. Whether I'd been interested in having her list my house if I decided to make an offer on this place.

"You know," I said. "When I think back, I remember how excited you were. Understandably, that's a big award. But Garrett seemed to be a little, I don't know, surprised or unaware that you won."

She laughed. "That's funny you say that. I remember talking about it with my husband later that night. Garrett had been so distant all evening. Not connecting with any of us at the table, and we were all Bate Real Estate employees. Then he gave that hilarious speech. It was a funny night. And I'll never forget winning the award in front of all my peers."

"Real Estate *Agent* of the Year. And now, here you are showing me a house."

"Yes. Now how much are you willing to offer?"

I told her I would think about it. She pushed a little bit, displaying the sales skill that enabled her to win Real Estate Agent of the Year, and drive an Acura Legend, but backed off when I told her I was late for work.

My supervisor, Alex Melia, greeted me warmly when I knocked on his open office door at Cal Farm Insurance later that morning. He invited me inside and I sat, once again, in the chair across from his desk.

"How's the Bate investigation going?"

"You were right about his alibi. That seems almost impossible to disprove."

"Yeah, that's the deal breaker, isn't it? Give it another day or two. It was unfair of me to give you one of our toughest cases your first day on the job. If you want, I can give you something else instead. I have a customer slip-and-fall at Big Bag Super

Store that looks bogus. You could work with the lead investigator on that one, if you'd prefer."

Riding shotgun on a department store claim would be an easier way to rack up time and experience. I needed the hours to earn my license, and it didn't matter how I got them, but I wasn't a quitter. "No thanks. I have my teeth sunk into this one. And I don't feel like letting go of it—at least not yet."

"Let's give it a couple more days. If nothing shakes loose by then, I'll give you a new assignment."

9

"Did you find out anything?" I asked when Rubia answered the phone at the Say Hey.

"You need to work on your conversational management skills. A simple 'hey' or 'hi' is customary when I answer and say, 'you've reached the Say Hey.'"

"Conversational management. I can't believe you remembered something from your communication studies days. Very impressive."

"It's one of the four skills in constructivism theory."

"Now you're just showing off."

"And all this time you thought I was sleeping in your classes."

"I'm sure you were."

"Want me to rattle off the other three skills?"

"No. Now what did you find about Candy?"

"Candy Cane," she said. "You gotta like that name. Sweet and curvy and melts in your mouth. Very creative."

"Don't embarrass me."

"I think I already did."

"I'm waiting."

"Real name is Mandi Coupland. Twenty-five years old. Lives in midtown. She's working on a PhD in astrophysics and nuclear engineering."

"Are you serious?"

"No, just messing with you. She's pretty much a fulltime stripper, though she's taking one class at City College in cosmetology."

"How'd you find this out?"

"I know a guy who knows a bouncer at Showtime Starlets. Candy mainly works there but sometimes goes on the road for better paying gigs. San Francisco, Reno, sometimes Vegas."

"She's honing her craft."

"Yeah, honing her craft. I'll have to remember that one, professor."

"Did you get an address?"

"Cost me twenty bucks, but yes."

"I'll pay you back."

"Damn straight." She gave me the midtown address.

I headed to 28th Street, arriving at the Elms Apartments, a three-story complex built in a square with a swimming pool in the middle. It was nicely landscaped and well maintained. From the numbers on the apartments I passed on the ground floor, I guessed Mandi Coupland's place was probably on the far side of the pool, on the third floor.

A female voice floated through the door when I knocked. "Who is it?"

I held up my Cal Farm business card to the peephole. "Ray Courage, ma'am, with Cal Farm Insurance. I was hoping you might have a couple of minutes to answer some questions."

A lock clicked and the door opened about four inches, the door chain drawn tight just below her chin. "What kind of questions? I didn't file a claim or anything."

"Oh, it's nothing to do with you personally—"

"If it's nothing to do with me personally, then why are you here?"

"Well, maybe a little bit. I wanted to talk to you about Garrett Bate."

She shut the door, and I thought she was blowing me off. But a second later I heard the chain slide and the door opened. "Come in."

The apartment was well appointed with butter yellow walls in the living and dining areas. The living room was tidy and tasteful—a leather couch and two wicker armchairs, a glass-top coffee table between them. A small alcove inset on one wall provided space for a television, stereo speakers, and a flower arrangement. Not what I expected of a stripper; though, I had to admit, the chrome dancing pole in the living room and flashing strobe lights I'd anticipated were a bit farfetched.

"Very nice," I said of the apartment, settling into one of the wicker chairs, dashing the pole imagery from my mind.

She didn't look like someone who made a living taking her clothes off in her white socks, blue jeans, and baggy green sweater. I supposed I imagined her opening the door wearing a lacy red bra and a thong. I admonished myself for stereotyping exotic dance professionals and their taste in furnishings and clothing.

Mandi sat on the couch, both feet firmly on the floor as she leaned forwards. She had a "don't bullshit me" face, someone who'd seen it all, heard it all, done it all, and who had little sympathy for anybody not recognizing.

"How do you know I dated Garrett Bate?"

"It was in our file."

She raised an eyebrow. It was never good to be in a file. "Why are you asking about Garrett?"

"Do you still see him?"

Her eyes narrowed and her nostrils flared. "That bastard. No, I don't see him anymore. Not for over a year now."

"If you don't mind my asking, why did you two break things off?"

"Ask him. He just called me one day and said it was over. Out of the blue. Didn't give me a good reason, but I think he was just tired of me and decided to throw me away. He was like that. He'd be all in to something, like a new band, or a restaurant, or whatever. Then, after a little while, he wouldn't want anything to do with it. Like for example, he got all in to the Kings, bought season tickets three rows from the court. Cost a fortune. We go to four games and all of sudden, he says one day, 'I hate basketball' and stops going. Doesn't even sell the tickets. Just lets them go to waste."

I didn't know a lot about Garrett, but her characterization didn't surprise me. "Do you mind if I ask how long you two dated?"

"You never answered my question. Why are you asking about Garrett?"

"It's an insurance matter regarding his wife."

"Tiffanie? He hated that bitch. There's another example right there. When Garrett met me at the club and asked me out, I told him no way because he was married. He said he was going to leave her and wanted to be with me. Can't believe I fell for it."

"How long ago was that?"

She paused to think, rubbing her chin with her thumb and forefinger. "Must have been close to three years ago."

"So you were dating when his wife died?"

"Oh, yeah."

"Was Garrett noticeably upset when she died?"

She laughed. "He was pumped, are you kidding me? He said a divorce was going to cost him at least a million dollars and it wasn't fair. Part of me feels sorry for her. Maybe she wasn't as bad as Garrett let on."

"Let's talk about the divorce. Had Garrett taken any steps to divorce her?" Nothing in our files indicated that he had.

"No. He just used that line on me to get in my pants. He never even talked to a lawyer as far as I know. But Tiffanie had. At least that's what Garrett said."

"Tiffanie had started divorce proceedings?"

"I don't think she actually filed anything. He said that she told him she was going to."

I nodded and leaned forwards in the chair. Tiffanie might have sentenced herself to death the day she told Garrett of her intentions to divorce.

"Did you know that Garrett had taken out a life insurance policy on his wife for a million and a half dollars?"

"I didn't."

"Is there anything else you can tell me about Garrett and Tiffanie?"

"I knew he was pissed at her for sleeping with some guy up in Tahoe. She'd slip up to their vacation home a couple of times a month and do this guy. Thought Garrett didn't know. But he did."

"Did Tiffanie know about you?"

Mandi shook her head. "No, we were discreet. I didn't want to be *that woman*."

I thought about how to respond, knowing whatever discretion she'd practiced prior to Tiffanie's death stopped shortly after it.

"I know what you're thinking. A stripper dating a wealthy married man. I already was *that woman*. But at the time, I believed he was going to divorce her, and what Garrett and I had was real."

I believed her. I did. "Last question. Did Garrett ever say anything about killing his wife? Either before or after she died?"

She was silent for a long time. "He never said anything, but I thought about that as soon as it happened. Part of me thought he did it. That was when things were good between us, so I wouldn't let my mind go there. Now, yeah, I think it's possible. Like I said, he gets bored with things real fast and throws them away."

10

Instinctively, I believed Garrett Bate to be guilty of killing his wife. His alibi made that belief misguided, even foolish. The character of the man emerging during my brief investigation was of someone far from likeable. That didn't make him a murderer.

Amanda Bate seemed like a good person to talk to if I was going to understand her son. Always a shameless hussy, I'd capitalize on the spark of attraction that seemed to fly from her when we met earlier. At least, I hoped it was a spark of attraction and not a post-menopausal hot flash.

Truth be told, I didn't reveal to her I worked for Cal Farm Insurance, offering only that we'd met the day before in the parking lot, and I thought she might help with my real estate needs. Yes, I drew out the word "needs" to give it an extra syllable and a shot of throatiness. Like I said, hussy.

We agreed to meet at eight o'clock that evening at Arden Hills Tennis Club, where she had a regular weeknight match. She'd put my name on the guest list at the private club. I sat at a table in the bar and sipped a Bass Ale from a glass, waiting for her. The interior looked more like what you'd find at an upscale restaurant than a tennis club, the bar constructed of dark, heavy wood topped with white marble. Large original paintings adorned the walls, and every table featured a bouquet of fresh-cut flowers.

She arrived about a quarter past the hour, wearing a gray tennis skirt that fell well above mid-thigh and a short sleeved, sunset patterned top in which the zipper had been pulled down to her cleavage. Even at her age, she had a figure that would turn heads.

"Sorry I'm late. I was playing a challenge match for the club rankings and we had to go to tiebreaker. Took forever."

"Did you win?"

She smiled at me and put a hand on my forearm sitting atop the table. "Darling, I always win." She winked, a gesture suggesting she was either kidding or serious. I didn't know her enough to distinguish which. "I'm so glad you called." She kept her hand on my arm.

After setting the date to meet her, I'd spent all day trying to figure out how to play it with her, coming up with no good ideas. "Can I get you something to drink?" That was as far as my planning had gone.

"Vodka gimlet, double, straight up. Just tell the bartender to pour my usual and he'll know."

I returned with the stemmed gimlet glass in hand.

She sucked down half of it in two swallows and turned her attention to me. "How do you know Garrett?"

"I don't really. We ran into each other in the parking lot and started chatting. That's when we saw you."

"I remember." She patted my forearm.

I smiled at her and drank some of my beer. "It was a shame what happened to his wife."

Her face slowly dissolved from upbeat and flirtatious, to something else altogether. She cast her eyes down and pressed her lips together. "I'm sorry. That still breaks my heart. To be taken at such a young age." She dabbed at a tear with her index finger.

We sat quietly for several seconds. "I certainly know how to throw cold water on a pleasant conversation," I said. "Let's change the subject."

"Good idea. So you said you're looking to make a move in the real estate market? Are you planning to relocate from where you are? Or are you a speculator?"

I didn't want to play the same game with her as I had with Gracie Nixon. I didn't mind being a little deceitful, but I wanted to at least give the deceived a different line of bullshit. Even us shameless hussies have standards. "Let's not talk business, not yet, anyway. I also thought it would be nice to meet you socially."

"Here's to that." She raised her glass and took another big swallow, leaving only a remnant of vodka and lime juice.

"Another?"

"Sure." She polished off the rest of the drink.

I ordered a drink for her and another Bass for me. This time we clinked glasses.

"So, I don't know a thing about you, other than you were talking to Garrett yesterday. Who are you, Ray Courage?"

I gave her a true rundown of my biography up to, and including, my retirement from Sacramento State. At the moment,

I told her, I was between careers, but was enjoying my retirement until I figured out the next stage in my life.

She nodded and raised her glass to me. "To your next stage."

"Now it's your turn. Tell me about you."

"Short version or long version?"

"Long version will give us more time to drink."

"Here, here." She raised her glass again, and I reciprocated.

She was born and raised in Sacramento, married her high school sweetheart, divorced her high school sweetheart after fifteen years of marriage, and never wanted to tie the knot again. "I like men, don't get me wrong," she said with a wink. "But I don't ever again want the pressure of making someone else happy day in and day out."

The comment gave me pause. Maybe that was why I'd never become a successful entrepreneur, real estate tycoon, or corporate executive. I lacked the drive to put business before family. I enjoyed making my wife, Pam, happy; cherishing the moments I could cook her dinner or surprise her with a gift or special night. I believed in my heart Pam felt the same. God, I missed her.

Amanda continued her story. After she and her husband graduated from Sac State, they started working for Coldwell Banker Real Estate before opening Bate Real Estate five years later. "We were successful right from the start. Maybe too successful. We both became addicted to the business, and before long, we started neglecting each other. We divorced when Garrett was twelve."

"I'm sorry."

She waved off my comment. "Long time ago."

"Where's your ex-husband now?"

"They moved to Salem. Up in Oregon. My ex had some contacts up there and thought it would be a good place to start a new real estate business. We agreed it would be best for one of us to leave town so we weren't in competition. He graciously agreed to be the one to leave. He's a big golfer, and there are lots of good courses around Salem. So it's been a perfect fit for him."

"You said 'they' moved to Salem. Who are they?"

"My husband, Alexander, and my other son, Jake. We let the boys choose which parent they wanted to live with. Garrett chose me, and Jake wanted to move up to Oregon with his dad. To be honest, that hurt my feelings a little bit, but I understood. They were different. Garrett and I connected more than his brother and I did. Same with Jake and his dad."

We ordered one more round of drinks. Amanda's hand went from my forearm on top of the table to my knee underneath it. A couple more drinks and this cougar would pounce. I was too long in the tooth for typical cougar prey, but I was getting the feeling she'd soon feast on anything male.

After we polished off the round of drinks, I insisted on coffee for both of us before driving. Then I walked her to her car.

She leaned in for a kiss, and we did so for a few seconds before I broke it off.

"Want to stop by for a nightcap?" she asked.

"Some other time," I said, feeling both guilty for lying and my stir of libido at the attraction I'd felt for her. Hussiness was a tricky thing to manage.

11

The next morning, the drive west on Highway 50 took me across the Sacramento River, the recent rains swelling the slow-moving waters to within a couple of feet of the levee's top. A good rainstorm might push the water over the brim, a constant concern in a city the Army Corps of Engineers characterized as the next New Orleans waiting to happen. The first exit across the river was Jefferson Boulevard, which I took south about three miles, arriving at the address on Partridge Avenue just after nine.

Though West Sacramento had undergone an urban makeover in recent decades, this part of town remained rural. Many of the residents who lived in the small farms and ranches refused to identify their location as West Sacramento, preferring Southport, the area's name in a bygone era.

Tiffanie Bate's childhood home sat at the end of a gravel driveway about fifty feet from the street. Two old pickup trucks and a newer Camry were parked on the driveway. The front yard consisted of several raised planter boxes with a variety of vegetables thriving in the wet fall weather, along with several large oak and maple trees shading the house. The side and back yards encompassed a couple of acres, home to at least the two horses and three goats I saw corralled inside the wire and wood fence.

I parked up the street and approached the house, a small ranch style home, painted white with light blue trim. It was a place suggesting solid, middle-class America.

"You the fella that called?" a man asked, emerging from an opening screen door before I'd reached the porch. He was a big man with a big belly and a round head.

"Ray Courage."

"I'm Frank Fields, but you can call me Papa. Everybody does. Come on in."

I followed him through the living room to the kitchen where a gray-haired woman in jeans and a long-sleeved cotton shirt was loading the dishwasher.

"This is my wife, Doris. Doris, this is the guy who called earlier."

She nodded, looking at me warily, a profound sadness unmistakable in her eyes. I smiled and introduced myself. She nodded again and returned to the dishes, turning her back to me. The old Ray Courage charm at work yet again.

"I've got some chores to get done, so I hope you don't mind talking while I work," Papa said.

I followed him through the kitchen door to the back yard. We walked along a crushed granite path bisecting the dirt yard and leading to a large barn at the back. The two horses watched us as we passed.

"Look at 'em. They know they're gonna get fed."

We reached the barn, where Papa hoisted a pitchfork and began loading oat straw and long strands of green grass into a large wheelbarrow.

"Okay, now that the missus isn't within earshot, tell me what this bullshit is about the insurance company taking a second look at my daughter's death." He stopped loading the hay and regarded me, jaw clenched. All of a sudden, homespun Wilford Brimley turned into Al Pacino. He now seemed as tough as a two-dollar steak.

"We just wanted to see if anything new might turn up. I don't mean to upset you or imply that we have anything, but we wanted to take a fresh look."

"You're not answering my question. If you're saying that you think that slime ball husband of hers killed my daughter, then I'm all ears. I've been saying that from day one. Just nobody can prove it."

"I'm looking at that, yes."

"But you said you don't have anything new?"

"Not really. There are some things that I want to explore further, so I can get a better picture of things two years ago."

"Like what?"

"For one, I'd like to know more about Garrett and Tiffanie. How did they meet? What was their marriage like?"

He resumed loading the wheelbarrow. "Have you seen my daughter?"

"Pictures." In addition to the accident-scene photos, there were two headshots of Tiffanie in the case file.

"So then you know she was a looker. Men were always chasing her. She loved that, always leading them on. Met that bastard at a polo match of all things. Fundraiser that her company sponsored, and she liked horses and all. She was serving wine, and this Garrett sees her, and next thing you know they're dating. A year later they were married."

"How long were they married?"

"When she died, it was just after their fourth anniversary," he said, his voice cracking. He shot a hand to his mouth and blinked back tears. "Sorry. It still hurts. I still can't believe it."

"I understand. I'm so sorry. My apologies for bringing this up all over again." I bit my lower lip, feeling the man's grief. I'd lost my wife. He'd lost his daughter. Even years later, the pain from such tragedies sometimes hit so hard it almost doubled you over. Tiffanie had been a real person, but all I had were a couple of photographs, descriptions of her on paper, and a summary of what caused her death. Now I saw how her life touched others, the people who loved her most. Her life had given her parents joy and love; her death had banished those emotions, leaving behind only emptiness, an emptiness that could never be refilled.

New tears came and several seconds passed before he composed himself, wiping his eyes with the top of his sleeve. "If it means you'll nail him, then I have no problem with you bringing it up. What else do you want to know?"

"How would you characterize the marriage the years they were together?"

"The year before they were married, and the first year or so afterwards, were good. Tiffanie seemed truly happy." He shook his head, slowly, as if recalling some image from the past. "My wife and I never liked him. He was arrogant, thought we were a couple of stupid hicks living out here like we do." He stopped using the pitchfork and stuck it in the ground in front of him. "About six months before…before it happened, Tiffanie came home to see us. She was crying. Said she thought Garrett was cheating on her and didn't know what to do about it. We told her to talk to a divorce lawyer then tell Garrett she wanted a divorce."

"Did she do that? Talk to a lawyer and tell her husband?"

"Yep. Sure did."

"Did she tell you what Garrett's reaction was?"

"She said he wouldn't let her divorce him. He did say he'd stop seeing the other woman. I don't know that he did or not, but Tiffanie didn't go through with the divorce, at least not at first.

Then she started seeing that carpenter up in Tahoe. We found out about it and told her to stop. But she said he treated her really well, not at all like Garrett did. I suppose in a way, it helped her confidence. She said now that she had someone who loved her, she could go through with the divorce and move in with this boyfriend."

"Do you know if she told Garrett the second time about wanting to divorce him? You know, after she started seeing Harley Cowan?"

He shook his head. "No idea. We never talked with her again after she told us her plans."

"One last question, and I'm sorry if it's a little indelicate. Whatever became of Tiffanie's engagement and wedding rings?"

He snorted. "Garrett got them. We never even thought about them. Then the SOB had them delivered to us a couple of weeks after the funeral. UPS truck drives up one day, brings us a small box. Inside are the two rings. No note or anything. I don't know why he'd do that. We didn't know if he thought we wanted them for sentimental reasons, or if we wanted to sell them, or if he was thumbing his nose at us. We never could figure it out. He knew we hated his guts, so he never called or contacted us to explain."

That puzzled me for a moment, then it made perfect sense after I turned it around in my head. "What did you end up doing with those rings?"

"I threw them in the God damned river. They didn't remind us of Tiffanie. They reminded us of him."

12

I caught the eleven fifty-five Southwest flight from Sacramento to Portland, touching down in Oregon on schedule at one twenty in the afternoon. I toted an overnight bag to the Enterprise Car Rental counter, though I hoped to be able to fly back to Sacramento later that afternoon. I'd promised Rubia I'd relieve her at the Say Hey and close it for the night, saving her from a thirteen-hour day behind the bar.

I was used to driving my compact Japanese sedan in Sacramento, but the only car left on the Enterprise lot was a black Dodge Charger. At first, the car seemed too beefy and unwieldy. After driving it several miles, I started to enjoy its horsepower, unabashed masculinity, and rich aroma of new car and leather. I cranked up George Thorogood and the Destroyers on the radio, pulled into the fast lane, and checked my sunglasses in the rearview. Ray Courage, Bad Ass Dude. Rubia would've taken one look at me in that car and fallen down in laughter.

Low, gray clouds stretched across the sky, patches of bright blue peeking through, here and there, as I drove south on I-5 towards Salem. I passed lush rolling hills packed with dense stands of trees, clicking by small town after small town. Crestwood. Lake Forest. Wilsonville. Donald. Northgate.

Highland. In the light afternoon traffic, the drive took less than an hour. The first order of business was lunch; my only meal thus far today had been an apple and cup of coffee I scarfed down before my nine o'clock visit with Tiffanie's parents.

I found a place called Cozzies, a sandwich spot run by a very engaging couple, Dave and Deb Cozzie. I ordered the bacon, lettuce, tomato, and avocado on sourdough. While I awaited my order, I browsed a bulletin board near the front door. A few apartments were listed for rent or to share, the rates much lower than the Sacramento market's. A Willamette University football schedule showed they had a game coming up against Linfield College. There were two flyers advertising an open-mic comedy competition in two days. I raised an eyebrow when I noticed one of the competition's sponsors was none other than Bate Realtors.

I devoured the sandwich and vowed that if I ever returned to Salem, I'd make Cozzies a regular haunt.

The state capital boasted scores of historic buildings dating back to the city's origins in the 1840s. Except for the new model cars on the street, I could've been in the middle of the twentieth, or even nineteenth, century. I parked downtown on Liberty Street, near the intersection at State Street, and walked halfway up the block, spotting the arched gilt lettering of Bate Realtors. The building was at least a hundred years old. The lower half of the two-story building was made of brick, punctuated with large picture windows under billowing brown canvas canopies. The windows afforded clear views inside several businesses housed in the quarter-block long structure. Through the glass at Bate Realtors, I could see five empty desks and an older man working at a desktop computer. On their front door, I noticed a flyer like the ones at Cozzies advertising the upcoming comedy competition.

The man looked up from the computer and gave me a friendly smile when I entered.

"I'm looking for Jake Bate. Do you expect him soon?" I surveyed the empty room, affirming that no one was making photocopies, returning from a restroom break, or otherwise engaged in the office.

"Do you have an appointment?"

"No, more of a drop in."

"He's my son. He went off to show a house about an hour ago. He should be back in a few minutes. Is there something I can help you with?"

"That's okay, maybe I'll come back in a bit." I was standing a few feet from his desk and noticed a framed photo on one side showing him and three other men holding golf clubs, the lettering across the bottom of the photo read "Illahe Hills Country Club Men's Scramble Champions."

"I knew I came to the right place," I said. "You play golf?" I recalled Mrs. Bate mentioning it the night before.

"Golfers play golf. Golf addicts live golf."

I laughed. "I've heard there's some great golf in this area, and was hoping to find someone who might have recommendations." When I retired, I'd considered taking up the game again. I'd been a decent collegiate golfer, but in the ensuing years, work and family duties had eased me away from the game.

"Illahe Hills." He pointed at the photo. "That's private, of course. You have to be a member to play there. But there are several public courses I'd recommend. My favorite is Salem Golf Club. Beautiful course. Tough but fair. Been around since the 1920s."

"Thanks for that. I'll look into it."

"You said the next time you were up this way you'd like to play. Where you from?"

"Sacramento."

"No kidding." He stood, walked around his desk, and came over to shake my hand. "Alexander Bate. I'm originally from Sacramento. I loved it there. Though, I don't miss the summers." He was as tall as Garrett and even better looking, with a lion's mane of shiny gray hair, and an infectious sparkle in his eye.

"But it's a dry heat," we said in unison, reprising a common Sacramento expression used to justify one hundred and five degree temperatures. We both laughed.

"No, I love it up here. It's home now. Has been for a while, ever since my son and I moved here, we've been comfortable."

We'd run out of small talk, an uncomfortable silence settling in, when I looked at Bate's desk again and noticed yet another flyer for the comedy contest. I pointed at it. "I see you're sponsoring the local comedy event.Is it a big deal?"

"Kind of. We've been sponsoring it for a couple of years now, right after Jake won three years ago."

"Your son won the comedy competition?"

He nodded. "Yeah. He's won it the last three years in a row."

"Is he a professional comic?"

"No, nothing like that. He works here fulltime. Comedy's just kind of a hobby. He's always been a strong public speaker with a good sense of humor, so he gave it a try a few years back, and he keeps winning the damn thing." Alexander Bate shook his head and smiled. "Hey, speak of the Devil. Here he is right now. Just talking about you, buddy."

I turned around to look behind me as young man approached from the front door. I could feel the color drain from my face, my mouth suddenly dry. Standing in front of me was Garrett Bate. Same height. Same build. Same face. Same haircut. Same taste in clothes. The only small difference I detected was a pink scar, about an inch long, on the side of his chin.

"You know, I never did catch your name," Alexander said.

"Ray Courage." My voice almost betrayed my shock.

"He's from Sacramento, Jake."

"Cool. Welcome to Salem. Are you looking for a new home up here?"

"Not exactly, no." I was muttering as my mind was shuffling through a mental deck of note cards.

"Are you okay?" Jake asked. He had Garrett's deep voice.

His question snapped me back to the moment. "I've seen you before."

"You have? Really? Do you remember where?" Though he had Garrett's Hollywood looks, his eyes exuded a warmth Garrett's lacked.

"I do. It was a couple of years ago. I was at the Sacramento Realtors Awards Night at the Crocker Art Museum with my girlfriend at the time. You gave the keynote address. You were very funny."

He smiled. "Yeah, that was great. I—" He stopped suddenly, and his face reddened. "No, that wasn't me. I've never spoken in Sacramento. I thought you said the Salem Realtors Awards. You probably saw my brother. We're identical twins and he's in the business down in Sacramento. That must've been who you saw."

13

When I returned to my house about six thirty that evening, I went immediately to the case file in my office to confirm what I already knew—there was no mention of a twin brother in any of the reports. No mention of the father. Scant mention of the mother, only a note that she and Garrett worked in the same office.

Despite my excitement about the discovery of a twin brother and its implications, I was dead tired. I called Rubia and told her I needed a couple hours sleep, but would be at the Say Hey at nine to take over her shift. The evening had turned cold, so I dialed up the thermostat and poured myself a snifter of Remy Martin cognac. I downed the cognac and poured myself another half snifter. I set the alarm on my cell phone for eight thirty, and after finishing the second drink, kicked back in my favorite leather chair, my feet propped up on the ottoman.

I drifted off before the effects of the second cognac had even set in. The past couple of days had been a whirlwind; such a change from my previous profession's day in and day out activities, I felt a bit off center. I contemplated what the past days had brought. Part of me was scared. Scared I couldn't finish the work, that I lacked what it took. I was also scared about the new territory I'd entered, one with people who did bad things to others. Another part of me felt excited that I'd broken free from my mundane life. There was also the sense of obligation I'd felt since I was a kid, the one pushing at the back of my mind, driving me to do right. It was this sense that led me into the investigative field.

A pleasant dream began to take shape. My wife was back with me, alive, smiling, just the way things had been…Then an army of hooded men burst into the house to take her from me. I couldn't move, helpless, as if someone held down my arms and legs.

Off somewhere in the distance, I heard an alarm trilling. Or maybe not an alarm at all. A phone? The sound faded, replaced by the angry snarling of a pack of dogs. They came streaming in through every window and door of my house, snapping and biting as I tried to escape. Again, the alarm sounded and stopped. I shook myself awake, to clear my head of the visions, falling back to sleep only to confront another horror—someone was holding me down, prying open my mouth, while another unseen person poured hot poison down my throat. I gagged and felt sick after they did so, standing and staggering. I vomited in hard, gut-wrenching waves until I had no more to purge. I collapsed and fell to the floor, turned to my side and looked out to see the chair and ottoman, the table light turned down low as I'd left it before my nap.

I wasn't dreaming. I'd become sick. Had someone poisoned me? The cognac? That was the last thing I could remember as my eyes closed, my head spinning so savagely I felt I might be thrown against the walls of my house. That was the last sensation I remembered before everything went black. Black, still, and so quiet. I lay in that state for what seemed an eternity.

"Ray! Ray! Ray!"

Someone patted my cheek insistently, while a second hand pressed against my jugular. Everything was blurry when I opened my eyes. I tried to focus on the person hovering over me, my hazy vision offering nothing better than triple vision of the figure.

"Are you all right?" The voice was Rubia's.

I shook my head, or at least I think I did. "Furnace."

"What?"

"Furnace."

"What?"

"Turn…off…the…furnace."

Rubia rushed from me to the thermostat. Then I could hear her opening windows and the front door.

"The paramedics are on their way. I called nine-one-one. Can you move?"

I nodded. She helped me up and led me outside. Holding me under one armpit, she lowered me to the top step of my porch so I could breathe in the fresh night air. A siren came into earshot, and soon, an overkill of fire trucks and an ambulance rolled in front of my house.

"How'd you get in?" I asked her after a few minutes.

"You gave me a key, remember?"

I looked at her and shrugged, my head too heavy and dull to remember anything. We sat together without another word until a guy in a uniform rushed up to us.

"I think it's carbon monoxide poisoning," Rubia said to the man. He immediately put a mask over my mouth and nose and turned a knob atop an oxygen tank. I felt a surge of fresh air and clarity, though I still felt shaky and nauseated.

In spite of my protestations, the paramedics hauled me off to Sutter General Hospital, where I'd spend the night in intensive oxygen therapy. Rubia rode with me and slept in my semi-private room, propped in a chair that reclined into something approximating a bed.

When I awoke the next morning, I had a small headache, but otherwise felt fine. The nurse brought in two pills for the headache when she delivered my bacon and eggs. Hospital food had improved since my last time visiting a friend years before. Starving as I was, I wolfed down the breakfast.

"Could have at least saved some for me," Rubia said, getting up from the recliner. She stretched and yawned, her eyes bloodshot.

"Figured you've already been to the cafeteria three times."

"Twice. But it's been almost an hour since the last time."

There was an awkward silence. Rubia worked at moving the chair back from reclining mode to the original configuration. She completed the task and sat back down.

"Thank you. You saved my sorry butt. How did you know I was in trouble?"

"When you didn't show up at nine, and then not at nine thirty, I knew something was wrong. That's not like you. I called about ten times. When you didn't answer your cell, I closed the bar down and went straight to your house. I used my key and saw you lying in the middle of the floor, a trail of puke from the chair to where you were flat on your face. Wasn't pretty."

"I can imagine."

"Kind of pushing the bounds of friendship, a scene like that."

We exchanged looks, saying nothing, conveying everything.

"Cop came in earlier while you were still asleep," she said, breaking the silence. "He said a PG&E inspector checked your furnace. Somebody had stuffed some insulation into something called the flue exhaust stack in your heater. There was a hole in it, too. That's what caused the carbon monoxide to escape. Cop said the paramedic told him that another twenty minutes, and you would've been dead."

I wanted to say something witty, but wasn't up to it. I felt crappy, and I was angry. I was up against someone who lived by values and beliefs outside the bounds of a decent society. This was someone who would do anything for his own self-interests. "I know Garrett Bate did it."

"The real estate dude that offed his wife?"

"Yeah." I told her everything I'd found out so far, up to, and including, learning he had a twin brother who lived in Salem.

"Sounds like you got him dead to rights," she said.

"No, not at all. I mean, I think I know how he did it. The problem is I can't prove it. Nobody can."

14

Rubia drove me home from the hospital. My head felt a little heavy, but the dizziness and nausea had ended. I went to the utility closet and examined the punctured flue. PG&E had taped a red danger card next to it, warning the furnace needed to be repaired by a professional and examined by a gas company technician before it could be operated again. The pilot light had been turned off, the inlet valve shut tight. A similar danger card had been affixed to my thermostat.

I checked all my doors and windows for signs of forced entry. Next to the outside doorknob on the French doors leading to the dining room, I noticed a small indentation on one of the doors where it met with the other door. It was as if someone had inserted a narrow screwdriver to push back the latch bolt. The indentation could've been old. I couldn't be sure. It didn't matter. I knew what happened.

I phoned Royle. He said he'd make a couple of calls and get back to me. While I waited, I called Alex Melia at Cal Farm to update him with the latest developments. I spent the rest of the morning making appointments with a security company for an alarm estimate, and with a heating and air conditioning company to repair my furnace. Just before noon, Royle called me back, and I was out the door.

After a brief meeting, I ate a light lunch of a green salad and glass of water at the La Bou on Howe. By now, my head was clear, and I felt my usual self. It was another foggy, cold day, the kind of day that made you pray for rain or sun. Anything but another day of fog and its soul-sapping dreariness. I was tired of the fog. The drive from La Bou to Fair Oaks Boulevard was just five minutes. Parking took a little longer, so by the time I walked into the Bate Real Estate office, it was almost two thirty.

The waiting and reception area were small, with only two guest chairs and a side table with several magazines fanned across it. A comely young receptionist was just sitting down at the desk carrying a mug, the string and paper label from a tea bag draped over the side.

"Can I help you?" she asked as she settled in to her seat.

"I'm looking for Garrett Bate." I added a smile to the pleasant tone I'd affected.

"He's in a staff meeting right now." She pointed to my right. Through a glass partition, I saw about fifteen men and women seated around a conference table. At one end of the table, Garrett was standing, running a PowerPoint presentation.

"Will it be much longer?"

"I'd say another hour. Would you like to come back, or would you like me to set up an appointment?

"I'll wait."

She didn't seemed pleased by me sitting ten feet away in one of the guest chairs as she drank her tea, though I kept my attention focused on Garrett in the next room. About ten minutes later, he finished his presentation. He turned off the projector with a remote and returned to his seat when he saw me through the glass. His face went ashen. He stood up, started to sit again, then stood straight up a second time. He said something in the direction of his mother at the other end of the table, and headed for the conference room door.

"What do you want?" he asked in an angry whisper when the door had closed behind him.

He stood over me as I flipped through a home and garden magazine. I let him stand there for several seconds. "You seem surprised to see me. I suppose I can't blame you for that."

"I, I…What do you want?"

"I'm thinking of redesigning my home office. What do you think of this style?" I turned the magazine so he could see the page. "You're in the business. You must've seen some very nice home office designs in your time."

"I think you should leave." He looked over his shoulder to see how much of this the receptionist was getting.

"I think we should go to your office. Unless you want to have this conversation right here."

His face was still frozen in shock. He looked into the conference then back at me. "Fine." He pivoted and started walking. I followed.

His office was in the back, past a cluster of open-air cubicle workstations and three enclosed offices. Amanda Bate commanded the largest office, in the far corner, while Garrett occupied the second largest office next to it. He shut the door behind us and closed the blinds covering the narrow window next to the entrance. He didn't sit and didn't offer me a seat.

"Cat got your tongue?" I asked.

"I don't know what you're doing here or why, but you can't just come into somebody's workplace unannounced—"

"Oh, cut the pretenses, Garrett. We both know you tried to kill me last night. And by that look on your face, you can't understand why I'm not dead."

"What?" He feigned ignorance, but he didn't pull it off.

"Stop! Let me tell you what I know." I made sure he was listening to me before I continued. I spoke slowly, making sure the gravity of each word sunk into him. "I met your dad yesterday up in Salem. Nice guy, your dad. Then I met your brother. Your identical twin brother, Jake. So, while I'm still up in Oregon, I'm betting Jake calls you, tells you a guy name Ray Courage came to visit. You figure I might be putting things together. About how maybe you had your brother stand in for you at the real estate awards while you were up in Tahoe. You can't take that chance. So you break into my house and mess with my furnace."

Garrett stood there, implacable, offering no objections, no false outrage.

"By the way, you should get a new MO. This furnace thing is so yesterday. Or should I say, so two years ago."

"Fuck you."

"Clever comeback." I took a step closer to him, to within an arm's length. "Let's jump to two years ago. You're upset that your wife wants to divorce you. Or, at least, you're upset that doing so will cost you a bundle of money. You can't just shoot her. Or do anything else that would point to you. So you decide to come up with what you think is the perfect crime."

"You think you're so sure about this. But you don't know. And you sure as hell can't prove it."

"You've got this identical twin brother. This lets you be in two places at the same time. Except for one thing. He's got this scar on his chin. He can't pass for you with that. So you both grow those god-awful chin beards so he can cover up his scar. Then you're identical again."

He was listening closely to every word, seeing how far I could take this.

"But I was watching the tape of that awards ceremony on YouTube the other night—thanks for the tip on that by the way—and noticed he wasn't engaged at all with his colleagues at the dinner table. That makes sense because he couldn't have the kind of inside conversations that only friends and colleagues can. He didn't even know Gracie Nixon, Real Estate Agent of the Year, was sitting next to him."

The color was returning to his face, and he pressed his lips tightly together as something started to smolder in his eyes.

"Then your brother gives a very entertaining and humorous speech, surprising everyone in the room. Seems you're not the comedian he is. After all, he's Salem's open-mic comedy champion for three straight years. I'm surprised he agreed to help you kill your wife, though. What was in it for him?"

He smiled, his face transformed from its previous anger to satisfaction. He knew I couldn't prove any of it. He seemed proud that someone had recognized his brilliance in planning and committing a crime no one could prove.

"I told him I was playing a practical joke on someone and needed to be somewhere else while this friend of mine had to think I was at the awards. He didn't ask any more questions than that. Afterwards, he might have suspected something, but we never talked about it."

"I could check the airlines to see if he booked a flight down here, before and after the awards ceremony."

"Don't bother. I was way ahead of you on that. He drove down."

"You're a sociopath. You're proud of what you did. Look at the smug look on your face."

"Bitch had it coming."

I leaned my face to within inches of his. "I'm going to the cops with this. They'll go after your ass. Even if they don't, Tiffanie's parents will have enough for a wrongful death lawsuit. The burden of proof there is much less than in a criminal trial. The publicity alone will destroy you." I backed off and let that sink in. "But you're lucky. Because I'm willing to keep my mouth shut about everything. About your twin brother and the switcheroo, all of it, for a measly fifty thousand dollars."

"You can't be serious. You don't have shit. I'm not paying you a dime. Those security cameras at the hotel have me in that hotel that night. And my friends will testify that I was with them up until that point."

"I have to admit, that was pretty clever. Jake saying he was too drunk to drive and had to stay at a hotel. Just so he could be caught on the security cameras to establish your alibi. Brilliant."

"Thank you. I thought so, too. He was sleeping in a nice two-hundred-fifty-dollar hotel room, while that bitch was dying with her lover boy." He laughed to himself, no doubt picturing his wife's lifeless body.

"About that. How could you be sure he was inside the house that night?"

"I didn't know if he'd be there at all. I was just trying to kill her. But the fact he was there was a bonus. He had it coming."

"One thing I haven't figured out is where you spent the night. Did you stay up in Tahoe?"

He shook his head. "No, I drove up early that evening, went in and did my thing on the furnace when they were out to dinner, and was back in Sacramento by ten that night. I parked my car five blocks from my house and snuck back home. No one saw me."

"You knew the police would look for a hired hitter, didn't you? That's why you sent Tiffanie's rings to her parents. So they couldn't speculate that you'd sold them to pay your hit man."

"Just being thorough. I would like to have sold off those rings and had a nice vacation. That would've been sweet justice, but it was more important to cover all my bases."

"I still want my fifty grand, or I'm going to the police."

"You're a pain in the ass. And you're not getting squat."

"Are you sure about that?"

"Yeah, dead sure. And a word of warning—I may have failed last night. But it won't happen again. You'd better look over your shoulder from now on."

I started to smile, even affecting a chuckle.

"What's so funny?"

I reached into the breast pocket of my shirt and pulled out my cell phone. "These things are amazing. You can take photos with them, send texts, e-mails, and do pretty much everything you can do on a computer. Ten years ago, none of this was possible. I remember when you had a home phone and a television with five channels. Now, you can carry a thousand times more than that in your pocket. Amazing. Hell, you can even transmit and record entire conversations."

"You recorded this?" He pursed his lips and brought a hand up to his mouth.

I nodded.

"Doesn't matter." His composure returned quickly." Nothing I said can be used against me."

"You didn't hear me. I didn't just record it. I was transmitting it to someone. Someone with a court order."

"You're bluffing."

Beyond his closed door, we could hear loud voices and a woman yelling. A few seconds after the commotion started, Garrett's door burst open, and the office filled with cops.

I held Garrett's gaze, his eyes filled with hatred, when the police cuffed him and read him his rights. He finally broke eye contact with me as a cop patted him down.

"Have a nice day," I said to him, and I walked out of the office.

Twenty or more employees stood in hallways, cubicles, and at office doors in stunned silence, watching the events unfold. I saw Royle approaching.

"Did you get everything?" I asked, holding up my phone.

"Yep. Once Sac PD books him, they'll transfer custody to us in a couple of days."

I walked out to the cold grayness towards my car. Inside, I dropped my head into my hands and rested my forehead against the top of the steering wheel. I stayed like that for more than an hour, letting the afternoon fade away until the outside cold seeped inside my car, chilling me to the bone. I started the engine and drove off. Tomorrow would be different for me. It wouldn't be different and better, or different and worse. It would just be different.

The past four days became a scrambled mess in my head, as if someone had put all my thoughts and emotions into a blender and turned it on high. I knew better than to try processing it all as I drove. It couldn't be done. To get a sense of what had just happened, and its far-reaching effects on me and everyone else, might take weeks or months. Or I might never know what I felt about bringing a killer to justice while his victim still lay dead.

The only thing I knew for sure was that there was no turning back.

The End

More Ray Courage

Available now on Amazon and other online retailers

Courage Matters

Ray Courage is asked by "Stockbroker to the Stars" Lionel Stroud to investigate an employee who's been acting suspiciously. Ray soon learns that not everything is as it appears at Stroud's firm. When his investigation uncovers a possible Ponzi Scheme orchestrated by Stroud himself, two people are murdered and Ray becomes Suspect Number One. Ray needs to find answers fast to avoid prison ... or death at the hands of the killer. Complicating his efforts are threats from a Mexican drug lord, hostility from a millionaire with a penchant for strippers, harassment from a cop bent on putting Ray away for life, and a rekindled love affair with Stroud's daughter.

Courage Resurrected

Ray Courage's wife Pam died thirteen years before in a car accident. Or did she? Ray receives e-mails from someone claiming to be his dead wife, accusing him of attempting to kill her and vowing revenge. As he deals with the possibility that his wife is still alive, he tries to find who's behind the threatening messages. As he does, Ray must outrun the police and elude a murderous predator.

www.ingramcontent.com/pod-product-compliance
Lightning Source LLC
Chambersburg PA
CBHW020550130626
46552CB00007B/2833